LUCKY GIFT

LUCKY GIFT

DONNA WILKES

Columbus, Ohio

The views and opinions expressed in this book are solely those of the author and do not reflect the views or opinions of Gatekeeper Press. Gatekeeper Press is not to be held responsible for and expressly disclaims responsibility of the content herein.

Lucky Gift

Published by Gatekeeper Press
2167 Stringtown Rd, Suite 109
Columbus, OH 43123-2989
www.GatekeeperPress.com

ISBN (paperback): 9781662902352
eISBN: 9781662902369

Library of Congress Control Number: 2020940739

Dedication

To my husband, Steve, I dedicate this book. Thank you for sincerely supporting my dreams and goals and being man enough to want me to go for them. I respect you for being so dedicated to your efforts and contributions toward this project. You bring such spice to my life. Love you forever!

Contents

Acknowledgments   ix

Chapter 1 New Beginnings   1

Chapter 2 Bus Station   9

Chapter 3 Passengers   13

Chapter 4 Cookies and Travel   17

Chapter 5 Fabulous Pizza   21

Chapter 6 Missing Book and Money   25

Chapter 7 Police and Cookies   31

Chapter 8 Medical Emergency   37

Chapter 9 7-Eleven   49

Chapter 10 Hospital and More   57

Chapter 11 Departures   65

Chapter 12 Business Heightens   71

Chapter 13 The Future   77

Chapter 14 Edith's Ultimate Oatmeal
Chocolate Chip C●●KIES   87

Acknowledgments

A special thanks to my daughter, Lori Barnes, my granddaughter, Olivia Barnes, and my dear friend, Anna Marie Kotsen, for their continued support in reviewing and the initial editing of this book.

I wholeheartedly thank my son, Steven Wilkes, my daughter-in-law, Cory Wilkes, and son-in-law, Hank Barnes, for their encouragement. In addition, the continuing inspiration from my grandchildren Josi, Noah, Olivia, William, Gabi, Izzie, and Asher.

Special acknowledgement to Lucky and Mitzy Deines, two inspiring dogs.

CHAPTER **1**

New Beginnings

This story begins in Memphis, Tennessee, because Michael and Jordan graduated from the University of Memphis. When Michael and Jordan first met in a computer science class, they were assigned to be lab partners, but they couldn't agree on anything. On many days they didn't even want to be in the same room with each other, much less be partners. They went through several rough spots. Then, about midway through their freshman year, things intensified.

One day, Michael decided to change the password on the lab files, where he and Jordan stored all their notes. Not knowing the password would prevent Jordan from accessing the lab data. When Jordan realized what Michael had done, he knew that wouldn't hold him back. Jordan retrieved and reset the previous password, which restored his access to the data.

Michael was impressed by how Jordan handled this situation. He also recognized how knowledgeable Jordan was and his strong technical capabilities. After that, Michael referred to Jordan as the technical genius on their team. Throughout the year, they realized they had a lot in common, especially their goals and dreams. Once that revelation occurred, their creative juices started flowing, and things just seemed to come together.

Jordan graduated with a bachelor of science degree in computer science, while Michael received a bachelor of science degree in technology management services. After graduation, both their families expected Michael and Jordan to return to their respective homes, but the graduates loved Memphis and were determined to make their new beginning in this city.

Soon after graduation, Michael and Jordan established a company, M&J Technology, which focused primarily on an invention they had developed.

To get their company started, they acquired a business loan, which allowed them to lease a small space and hire three employees. Their business resided on the fourth floor of an old brownstone building located off Riverside Drive, which overlooked the Mississippi River. Most days during lunch breaks, Michael and Jordan would sit and watch cargo transported by tugboats pushing large barges down the river. Some people joked that they could almost reach out and shake hands with the people of Arkansas because the state line of Tennessee and Arkansas was right down the middle of the river. Jordan and Michael would laugh that during their college years, they might have spent half of their time in the casino in West Memphis, Arkansas.

The beauty of brownstones in the area is they all have a unique story that goes with each one. In Michael and Jordan's building was a business known as the

Italian Pizzeria. Opened in 1925, the place was located on the ground floor. This place's claim to fame was that it put a twist on regular pizza with a Southern pizza style. The pizzeria used to be a popular local hangout for workers from the shipyards, who would often come for a pint and a slice. Rumor was that the smell of garlic had permeated the building even years after it closed, though not so much now.

Michael would often talk about one day owning this entire building because it was the perfect location. This area of Memphis is known as the crossroads of America within the transportation industry. At this location, Michael and Jordan were able to manufacture and distribute their products very efficiently.

Michael and Jordan both were handsome men, but Michael was the one who had the most outstanding personality. Jordan would joke Michael had never met a stranger. Jordan, on the other hand, just wanted to keep his nose to the grindstone. The combination of the two of them seemed to be very successful. Michael and Jordan were creative and had a great desire for their business to succeed quickly. The company came before girls, socializing, and even family.

The foundation for their business was an invention, a clear tracking strip that could be placed on any type of surface, object, or body. Since it was clear, it would not be readily noticeable, yet it could be tracked all over the world. The tracking method was by way of an app implemented on any cell phone, computer, or tablet device. As an example, parents could stick a tracking strip on their children, and only a special release cream could remove it.

Jordan often spoke about how this device could assist in locating lost or stolen children. Quickly finding lost children was important to him because when he was a teenager, his younger sister got separated from the family while they were at an amusement park. He said that it only took seconds, and she was gone. Situations like that made this product extremely valuable, even priceless. Each time Jordan shared this story, you could feel and hear the sense of panic, turmoil, and anguish in his voice. Fortunately, his sister was eventually found, but that event made a life-changing impact on him.

In the early development of the M&J products, there were multiple phases. Many test strips were produced for beta testing, along with several special strip-removal creams. Additionally, an internet app called "JAM" was created, which provided universal tracking technology. All of these components were necessary for completing this tracking application.

Michael and Jordan had already applied for a patent of their invention. The patent process is never quick, and in this case, it took what felt like an extraordinary amount of time. Initial indications looked very promising. The development of the tracking strips had progressed to a point where they required additional funding to be able to continue moving forward with product development and manufacturing. That's why Michael decided to travel to Kansas City. He planned to attend an entrepreneurial trade show on April 19,

2010, at which he could meet and share products with potential investors. He and his business partner felt like they were now in a position to pursue private investor funding for their company instead of bank loans. Of course, Michael could ask his family for financial support, but he and Jordan wanted to be independent and to manage their business on their own.

Michael's family was deeply rooted in the bourbon distillery business. His great-great-grandfather had started his first distillery over 175 years ago. Today, the distillery was still known as Bell Blended Bourbon (*BBB*), located in Midway, Kentucky, right in the heart of bourbon country. That was where nearly everyone Michael knew lived. His father and mother were real entrepreneurs that grew the business from a small bourbon shop to one of the most famous distilleries on the Bourbon Trail. Their bourbon had changed over the years, evolving into the perfect blend, and the profits reflected that. Michael often said he hoped he could live up to his family's expectations.

On the other hand, Jordan's family was modest, very loving, and down-to-earth. Both of his parents worked their dairy farm, night and day, as did Jordan's older brother and younger sister. Their dairy farm was also in Kentucky. A couple of times, Michael went home with Jordan and experienced what a family lunch really meant. These family lunches always included every family member when possible, and Jordan was very close to each one personally. Most of the food was grown right in the family garden on their land; even the fried chicken was made from their own chickens. Michael would comment that he hoped one day his wife could cook like Jordan's mom.

Jordan told Michael that when he made it big, he wanted to give back to his parents. He knew they had always worked so hard for what they had. The funny thing was that the family farmland they lived on was probably worth millions, but it would never be sold.

For right now, Michael and Jordan needed to focus on the trade show Michael was about to attend. Michael loved placing the tracking strips on items he carried around, so of course, he put one on the inside of his suitcase and on a book he was taking on his trip. Each strip had a unique code, which could identify where and what the tracking strip was associated with.

Michael found the perfect one-way bus ticket and left the return trip open-ended. He wanted to make sure he would be available if some investors wanted to stay over and discuss the products and opportunities in-depth. Michael scheduled a departure at 8:00 a.m. so that he would arrive around 5:15 p.m. This trip had no connecting transfers, but it did allow for a lunch and bathroom break. He would need to leave the office no later than 7:00 a.m.

Michael usually got to the office by 6:00 a.m. each day, when things were quiet, and he could focus on work without any disruptions. He especially liked coming in early during the springtime in Memphis.

The air was crisp, and birds would swoop down the river and rest on the boats to sing.

Things were different on the morning that Michael was preparing to leave. Atypically, Michael arrived late at the office. Jordan wouldn't be coming into the office because he always went to church on Sunday mornings. There had been an early morning downpour, which inevitably caused traffic jams. So, Michael had already arranged for a car to pick him up and take him to the bus station.

Michael informed the car driver that he was catching a bus to Kansas City, and it was departing at 8:00 a.m., so he would need a pick-up at 7:00 a.m. When the car arrived, Michael noticed the vehicle was an older model but appeared to be well-maintained. The driver got out and opened the door to the back seat for Michael. He confirmed with Michael that he was going to Kansas City.

Michael quickly got into the back seat with his briefcase full of tracking strips, his laptop, and other M&J business materials. The driver then placed Michael's suitcase in the trunk, and it seemed to take longer than usual. As the driver got back into the car, he explained his wife had put some things in the trunk that he'd had to rearrange. Michael noticed a picture of the driver's family on the dashboard, and he commented on how exceptionally clean the interior of the car was.

The driver was friendly, engaged in small talk, and reconfirmed the destination a second time. Once more, Michael told him that he was going to Kansas City. The trip went smoothly, and the driver got him to the bus station in little time.

CHAPTER 2

Bus Station

When Michael arrived at the bus station, it was darker outside than usual because of the overcast skies. You could see the bus station's neon lights illuminating the area. After pulling up in front of the bus station, the car driver sprang out of the car and grabbed Michael's bag from the trunk. He assisted Michael by carrying his luggage all the way up to the ticket counter; not every driver is willing to get out into the rain. Michael thought he should give the driver a nice tip for his eager service.

Michael noticed that the station was not overly crowded with passengers. Of course, there were a few waiting for their bus or a transfer. Others were seeking shelter and had come in from the rain. The station's emptiness also might have been due to it being Sunday morning, when a lot of people are attending worship services. This Sunday morning was shaping up to be an excellent time to travel.

Michael went directly to the ticket counter to check in. He showed the ticket agent his driver's license photo ID and the ticket information he had purchased online.

The ticket agent informed him this bus was the only one leaving today for Kansas City, Missouri. The agent was required by law to inform Michael that an ex-con would be traveling on this particular bus. She went on to encourage him not to worry; a prison officer would be riding along. Michael said it wouldn't bother him; he wanted the ticket anyway. It was vital Michael attend this trade show. He was glad he wasn't driving himself, what with the downpour.

The ticket agent asked him all the customary travel questions; then, she took Michael's luggage and passed it through to be loaded onto Bus 208. She gave Michael his boarding pass with his reservation number and baggage tag, then told him to proceed to the escalator and down to Dock 7A. Bus 208 was his bus, and it was currently boarding. He would need to hurry as the bus was preparing to leave soon.

As Michael passed through the bus station, he all of a sudden got an uneasy feeling someone was following him. He decided to stop in the men's restroom just to test his premonition and dry off a little bit. After doing this, things seemed to be all right. No one followed him into the restroom. He needed to hurry because he surely didn't want to miss his bus.

Michael proceeded quickly through the upper area of the bus station and down the escalator to the bus bay area. The configuration of this bus station was well-designed, with a large roof enclosing the entire bay area. It worked whether it was a hot and sunny day or pouring rain like today. Even so, bus diesel exhaust fumes filled the air.

Michael continued straight down the platform to 7A, where Bus 208 was parked. It appeared that Bus 208 was a reasonably new bus, which pleased Michael. Hopefully, this would mean there would not be any faulty bus issues or breakdowns.

Before boarding the bus, Michael presented the bus driver with the boarding pass the agent had given him, and a baggage tag to ensure his bag had been loaded. Michael then boarded and immediately glanced around. The smell of home-baked cookies permeated the bus. Wow, it smelled awesome. Michael could almost taste them!

A middle-aged woman was on his right as he started down the aisle of the bus. She had several boxes, apparently filled with cookies, on the seat next to her. Even her smile to Michael as he passed by was sweet and friendly.

Then, OK..., right there in front, on his left, was a very large man who appeared to occupy the entire seat. You could tell he pumped iron. Michael thought he might be the ex-con and certainly didn't want to get into a disagreement with him. Michael continued to walk past the seats on the bus, noticing different faces, some smiling and others just nodding.

He found a seat towards the right rear of the bus directly behind two young Latino men, probably about Michael's age. They most likely were brothers. On the left side of the bus was a well-dressed middle-aged man with his son, who appeared to be in his early twenties. The older man looked very familiar, as if Michael had seen him before. The son and father were in a heated discussion. A few rows behind them was a couple, and she was pregnant.

A Mexican woman with her young son sat at the very back of the bus. Then there was another middle-aged woman who sat across the aisle from the young couple. There were twelve passengers, and the bus driver, totaling thirteen people on the bus.

As the bus backed up and pulled out, you could hear conversations starting.

CHAPTER **3**

Passengers

And so, began the journey. Michael was able to overhear and absorb a lot of information.

Michael finally recognized who the older man was. It was Dr. Robert Abernathy, a world-renowned heart surgeon who had appeared several times on television. Now, here he was on this bus, in deep conversation with his son, Edward. It seemed that Dr. Abernathy wanted his son to focus on becoming a doctor. Edward apparently had plans of his own for his future. Their discussion was very loud and heated. It appeared neither one of them was willing to listen to the other's point of view.

Seated a few seats behind the Abernathys were Alejandro and Victoria; they were in deep conversation, their eyes locked on each other. They seemed to be quite passionately in love. The lady seated across the aisle from them, Miss Sophia, appeared to know Alejandro, and kept calling him, "Prince." She most likely was doing this because he closely resembled the famous entertainer, Prince.

The young lady sitting in the back was Maria. She was accompanied by her son, Jayden. They both were keeping to themselves. Jayden had brought a soccer ball with him, and he kept rolling it around with his feet. Interestingly, Edward kept glancing back at Maria, obviously enamored with her. It was not difficult to notice why Edward was taken by her. She was stunning.

Then, in front of Michael, was Johnathan. He was one of two brothers, and he had just graduated college with a financial degree. Nathan, the other brother, was just beginning his residency in Kansas City, as an internal medicine doctor. They were deeply engrossed in conversation. Johnathan seemed to be frustrated that Nathan was making progress with his career, and was very concerned with figuring out what he was going to do to get his own career in gear.

After the trip was well underway, Michael remembered why he had chosen to take this bus. It was because the route would be so enjoyable. First, they would travel on the interstate to Jonesboro, where the bus would get off and take a local highway. Michael always loved to travel the back roads, and Highway 63 was definitely one of those routes. The bus would go through the flatlands and hills of Arkansas.

Sure enough, as they exited the interstate and entered Highway 63, the rain stopped, as if God just flipped a switch. Highway 63 was a well-maintained road, but it had a lot of curves as it moved through the outskirts of many small towns. The traffic seemed to be light, most likely because it was Sunday.

When Michael looked out the bus windows, he could see railroad tracks that ran along the right side of the bus, and then through bends in the road, it would run along the left side. He thought about M&J Technology and how there would be many bends in the journey while growing the business. He and Jordan just needed to stay on track and focus on developing products that moved their business forward into the future.

From Michael's side of the bus, you could see the Spring River, and the view of it was absolutely beautiful. When the bus passed through Mammoth Spring, Dr. Abernathy commented that he would like to visit there. He had heard the fishing was great. One of his friends had shared with him that he attended an Arkansas fishing tournament there every year. The trout fishing is excellent in those spring-fed waters. Dr. Abernathy said, "I guess I need to put that on my bucket list."

As they crossed over the Missouri state line, Johnathan hollered out to the bus driver, "When are we going to stop for lunch?"

The bus driver replied, "We'll be stopping about twenty-five miles down the road in West Plains at a place called Fabulous Pizza. I have mapped us there. It's a great pizza place."

Johnathan indicated he had heard of this place but had never been there. College friends of his had told him about the restaurant and said the pizza was terrific. The chatter throughout the bus indicated everybody was getting excited and hungry.

Michael told the bus driver, "Twenty-five miles. Better roll fast."

Johnathan then asked the lady in the front if she could share some of those awesome-smelling cookies. "Sure," she replied, as she was very proud of her cookies, and she held them up for the taking. Of course, everyone accepted at least one, including the driver and the ex-con.

As each cookie was taken, the lady blessed each person in her own way. Several of the passengers commented that these were absolutely the best cookies they had ever had. It was either they were getting hungry, or Edith had a special secret recipe. Edward told Edith she should sell her cookies. A cookie business was something Edith had contemplated and which would undoubtedly be in her future.

CHAPTER **4**

Cookies and Travel

Then Nathan blurted out, "Wonder if she poisoned these cookies?"

Michael was shocked and stopped eating the cookies immediately, as did others on the bus.

"What do you mean?" said Michael.

Nathan and Johnathan were aware Edith had been in prison for apparently poisoning her neighbor. Then the large African American man that was seated up front, without even looking around, said, "Edith . . . did you poison the cookies?"

She said, "No. No, sir."

Michael immediately questioned, "Who is he?"

Nathan replied, "That's Bishop James Burrell, the chaplain at the prison. In fact, they call him the 'pope of the people.' They say he's in line to become a cardinal."

Michael had now realized that Edith was the ex-con. Who would have ever thought that this sweet lady would have been incarcerated? The large African American man, who Michael thought to be the traveling ex-con, was, in fact, an officer and chaplain at the prison.

Oh my gosh, Michael felt so ashamed that he had made a terrible mistake, falsely assuming Bishop Burrell of being an inmate. Michael thought he might like to talk to the bishop and apologize. He also felt he could use some special prayers for his trade show.

As the bus traveled through the Missouri countryside, it gave Michael time to reflect on all the things he had gone through over the past few years. He thought of his father, their relationship, and how Michael had wanted to make his dad proud. Building a company from scratch and developing products had placed a lot of stress on Michael. He was excited and pleased that he and Jordan had progressed their company to this point. Hopefully, he would find at least one investor at this trade show that would join them in getting their product out the door.

It also occurred to Michael that there was something different about this bus trip. The bus driver didn't seem to be too bothered about keeping a tight schedule, and the passengers were having conversations as if they had a purpose in knowing each other. It seemed quite unusual because, usually, you don't interact with other passengers while riding a bus. Pretty much, you just stay to yourself.

Soon, the bus pulled up in front of Fabulous Pizza. The bus driver and Bishop Burrell wanted to stay on the bus and asked if they could have a pizza sent out to them. As everyone else exited the bus, they noticed a lot of the other shops and restaurants along the street looked deserted or closed. Yet, when they entered the restaurant, a friendly man greeted them and welcomed them to Fabulous Pizza. He directed them to a table already set up for eleven diners.

There were several people in the restaurant, and it seemed everyone was enjoying an afternoon out. The place was super inviting. The décor and ambience of the pizza shop had a classic Italian design, and everything looked nice and clean. The tables had solid red tablecloths with an overlay of an angled checkered red and white tablecloth. What made it a little unique was the sophisticated chandeliers hanging from the ceiling and an edgy brick wall which held the open-pit pizza oven.

To be honest, it was the aromatic smell of pizza that reassured the passengers the bus driver had picked the right place.

CHAPTER **5**

Fabulous Pizza

Michael took the seat at the head of the table, and to his left sat Nathan, then Dr. Abernathy, Edward, Maria, and Jayden. To Michael's right sat Johnathan, Victoria, Alejandro, Miss Sophia, and Edith. They all engaged in conversations as if they were family or friends. A female waitress came over to Michael and asked what she could get for them. Michael said, "We would like a couple pitchers of beer and a soda for the young gentleman at the end of the table."

The waitress replied, "We don't serve beer on Sunday, but I can get you sodas." Then another waitress swished by with two large pitchers of beer in her hands.

Michael said, "Well, what is that?"

The waitress replied, "Those are pitchers," and winked.

Michael looked at her and said, "Then we'll take three pitchers, four large special pizza pies, an IBC Root Beer, for here, and one large pepperoni pizza and two IBCs to go." Everyone at the table smiled and nodded in agreement with Michael.

Miss Sophia told the waitress that this would all be on one check, and she would take it. That made everyone happy.

Michael noticed a large stage with speakers and musical equipment set up in front of the restaurant. He asked the waitress, "Is there a band performing today?"

She said, "Not on Sundays."

The group continued their conversations. Alejandro and Victoria engaged in deep conversation with each other, as did Edward and Maria. Miss Sophia and Edith acted as if they were long-lost girlfriends.

Michael started up a conversation with Johnathan about business financing. Michael shared that his grandfather was a wise man and that he had advised Michael that in his business, he should cautiously advance one step at a time. "Don't always dwell on the future, or what might happen tomorrow," Michael's grandfather would say. "Just concentrate on making the next step successful." His grandfather always talked about RTM, which represented Risk, Time, and Money equals Reward.

All of this conversation intrigued Johnathan. He knew his passion was finance, especially working with the details of start-up businesses. He found it exciting, taking a business from the ground floor while soliciting and engaging with potential investors. This conversation gave Johnathan some great ideas for future opportunities.

Michael was taking in the conversation, enjoying the nuances of the restaurant, when a familiar-looking woman passed by the table. What?? She looked just like Michael's car driver's wife. How could that be? What were the chances of her being here in this same restaurant? It must be someone else who just looked like her.

Maria excused herself and Jayden to go to the restroom. As she was heading back to the ladies' restroom, to her total surprise, there were two men who resembled Don Henley and Joe Walsh seated in a booth in the back. Maria rushed past them, trying not to stare. When she and Jayden exited the restroom, they were no longer there. She thought, *Was that just my imagination?*

As Maria returned to the table, to her surprise, she saw the two men who looked like Don and Joe were performing on the stage. Yet Joe was on the drums, and Don was playing a mean guitar. It was almost like a dream come true. She then saw Edward stand up and walk towards her. He said to Maria, "Come join us," then smiled and proceeded to the stage. He sat down at the piano and began playing.

Edward was fantastic. He knew it, and everyone there knew it. Maria sat Jayden down at their table, and then she stepped onto the stage. She bent over to Edward, whispered something to him, turned her back to the crowd, and said something to Henley and Walsh. Then everything went crazy. It was surreal; the roof blew off the place with a classic song . . . "RESPECT."

It was so awesome, even the cooks from the kitchen came out to listen. Everyone was captivated by the music. When the jam went into a slow-dance song, several people got up to dance. The party was on. Even Alejandro and Victoria, pregnant and all, were dancing. Dr. Abernathy was in total shock as to how well Edward was performing. He confessed he had never heard his son play and was ashamed about that.

Meanwhile, on the bus, Bishop Burrell and the bus driver could hear the music being performed inside the restaurant. Bishop Burrell asked the bus driver, "Don't we need to break this up and get back on the road?"

The bus driver responded, "Bishop, there is one thing in driving Bus 208; you can't rush a miracle."

The bishop understood and smiled at him, leaned back, and decided to just enjoy the ride.

CHAPTER **6**

Missing Book and Money

Michael was enjoying this place, but paused and remembered why he was here. He decided to play around with the JAM app on his phone and try locating his suitcase and book. Yes, his suitcase was on the bus; but surprisingly, the book was in the trunk of a car, located a short distance from the bus. How could this be?

Michael decided to take the pizza and sodas out to the bus for the bus driver and bishop. That would allow him to check out where his book was located. As he did, he noticed an automobile a few parking spots up from the bus. The car looked exactly like the car that had brought him to the bus station. Strange. Michael felt sure something wasn't right. Now his spotting of the car driver's wife in the restaurant was beginning to make sense. Michael could not figure out why someone would be so interested in his book.

He boarded the bus to deliver the pizza and immediately started sharing this strange experience with the bus driver and Bishop Burrell. Michael told them about the peculiar actions of the car driver with his luggage in the trunk. Michael also shared that he felt he was being followed while in the bus station, and thought he saw his car driver's wife inside the pizza restaurant. He explained to them how the tracking strips worked and how he could see where his luggage and book were. Both men believed Michael and were curious about it.

Bishop Burrell decided Michael's luggage would need to be checked out. He also thought it might be less conspicuous if he went down below into the baggage area, instead of Michael, to check it out. They were all thinking they could be under surveillance.

Michael said, "Sure," and when Burrell got down there, he called the bus driver on his cell phone and said,

"There is a padlock on his bag."

Michael, overhearing the conversation, said, "No, there isn't."

There was a pause, and then the bishop said, "Now there's not."

Michael looked at the bus driver, puzzled, and the bus driver said, "Don't ask. You learn a lot of crazy tricks working in prison."

Then the bishop said, "Oh my, Michael, there are hundreds of thousands of dollars here. What's going on?"

Michael said, "Take a picture."

Sure enough, there were. In fact, a lot of the money was still in bank bundles. Michael said, "What are we going to do? Where did this money come from?"

Burrell said, "It sure looks like it could have been a bank robbery. Michael, do you know anything about this money?"

Michael said, "I have no idea how that money got there. I packed my luggage myself, at home, with only my clothes, book, and personal stuff."

Burrell said, "If this money is from a bank robbery, the robbers must have planned to get the money out of town by some other method than themselves, as in, using your luggage. They must have used you as a money mule."

Burrell thought up an idea to act like he was searching through the luggage compartment as if he was looking for something. If anyone was watching, this might attract the attention of the robbers and persuade them to retrieve the suitcase before someone else discovered the money. So, Bishop Burrell started removing some of the bags out onto the sidewalk, acting as if he had lost something. Sure enough, along came the car driver, walking past, and he skillfully slipped away with Michael's suitcase.

With the tracking strip still attached, Michael knew he would be able to track his suitcase wherever the car driver might go. The driver went directly to his car, exactly where Michael's book was located.

Michael then let Bishop Burrell know his trick had worked, and the conniving robbers had just retrieved their stolen money.

Michael immediately reported the situation to the police. He offered to help track the robbers down.

Michael explained how this had started with him and said that he could identify where the money was located through his tracking app.

By this time, everyone was leaving the restaurant and returning to the bus. Burrell and the bus driver loaded the luggage back onto the bus. The group thought it was weird that the luggage was being reloaded. They all were loudly rejoicing and cheering Edward and Maria's fantastic musical performance.

As Maria and Edward boarded the bus, Maria turned to Edward and asked if he wouldn't mind going back to the restaurant and getting her sweater. She had left it on her chair. Edward was pleased to do this for her. He left the bus and went to the restaurant. When he reached the front door, there was Maria's sweater hanging outside on the front doorknob. Now, this seemed strange.

Edward peeked through the front door and into the restaurant. He was shocked to see the restaurant looked as if it had not been open for business for many years. There was dust and dirt everywhere, and things were in complete disarray. He also noticed a "Closed for Business" sign in the front window. This made no sense. They all had, just moments earlier, been inside enjoying themselves. Indeed, this puzzled him. Edward hastily retrieved Maria's sweater and ran back to the bus, dumbfounded.

Upon entering the bus, he was distracted by everyone cheering and congratulating him on his piano playing and singing performance. With such excitement, Edward overlooked mentioning the strange fact of the restaurant they had all just been in was mysteriously closed. When he saw his father standing and blocking the aisle of the bus, smiling at him, Edward approached his father, who immediately put his arms around him. His father had not shown much affection towards Edward for a very long time.

Edward's father said, "I'm so proud of you," and kissed him on the cheek. Edward waved for Maria to come over and join them. She brought Jayden with her.

Edward said, "Dad, I would like for you to meet Maria Martinez, and yes, Dad, her family produces those awesome strawberries which you love. Maria, this is my father, Dr. Robert Abernathy."

Dr. Abernathy reached out his hand and greeted Maria. "Maria, that was a fantastic performance. Do you do that professionally?"

Maria smiled and said, "No, but I would love to." Maria pulled Jayden from her side and said, "Sir, I would like for you to meet my son, Jayden. He is seven years old and aspires to become a soccer player." She winked.

Dr. Abernathy reached out and shook Jayden's hand and said, "Nice to meet you, young man."

Edward and Maria continued to the back of the bus, but Jayden wanted to stay and sit with Dr. Abernathy. As they were seated, Jayden looked up at Dr. Abernathy and said, "Are you going to be my grandfather?"

Dr. Abernathy said, "I don't know, but right now, we can at least be good friends." Jayden smiled. The two of them began to discuss their favorite sport. Of course, soccer was Jayden's, and fishing was Dr. Abernathy's. Jayden shared that he had never been fishing and would like to do that one day.

CHAPTER 7

Police and Cookies

Not long after leaving the restaurant area, a police car approached with a blue light flashing, and a loud, high-pitched siren that sounded like "Waaaaaahhhhhh." Some of the passengers became alarmed when the police motioned to pull over—especially Jayden. He stood up to see what was going on.

Jayden, only being seven years old, had an imagination running wild. He turned around to Dr. Abernathy with a look of concern, as if the police were coming to get him. Dr. Abernathy comforted him. He told the boy to come sit down and reassured him that everything would be all right.

The policeman exited his car and stepped aboard the bus. He stated he wanted to talk to the bus driver, the bishop, and Michael. All this seemed concerning to the rest of the passengers. Michael, the bus driver, and the bishop, however, appeared to understand what was happening.

Upon boarding the bus, the officer remarked, "It sure smells good in here."

Edith smiled at him and said, "Sir, would you like a cookie?"

He smiled back and said, "Yes, I would!" Edith handed him a large cookie. The policeman thanked her and immediately began devouring the cookie. The officer asked the bus driver, Michael, and the bishop to disembark the bus.

As they exited the bus, the remaining passengers pushed up to the front of the bus to see what was going on. Edith sat in the driver's seat for a good view of the action. Outside, directly in front of the bus, the policeman began questioning Michael regarding the money and a possible robbery. The policeman, all of a sudden, began acting really funny, dancing around, and being very fidgety. The passengers on the bus were now extremely curious as to what the heck was going on.

Then, the bishop looked up at Edith, in the front window of the bus, and mouthed something about the cookie. Edith said to the group, "I don't think the bishop is happy about me giving the officer one of my hot pot chocolate chip cookies."

Everyone on the bus stared at Edith and began laughing. She had given the officer a marijuana cookie. Edith reassured them that she had a valid ID card to be able to legally dispense medical marijuana in multiple states, but not so much to unsuspecting police officers. Oops!! Hopefully, it would just give him a good rest.

Michael, the bus driver, and the bishop had to assist the policeman back to his vehicle physically.

They placed him into his patrol car, locked the door, and the officer kept hollering he wanted one more of those damn good cookies. They then quickly returned to the bus. The bus driver instructed everyone to hurry back to their seats. Once more, they sped down the road towards Kansas City.

Edith once again raised a cookie in the air and said, "Anybody want a cookie?"

Jayden immediately rushed up to the front of the bus to get his. Jayden asked if he could take one to his friend, Dr. Abernathy. And of course, everyone else wanted one as well. Bishop Burrell asked if his cookie had cannabis in it.

Edith said, laughing, "No, sir, I am saving those for the police." Bishop Burrell turned and gave her a raised eyebrow. Edith realized she had better tone down that rhetoric.

Some of this raised questions in Michael's mind about Edith and why she had been in prison. Michael asked Johnathan and Nathan if they knew the full story behind Edith's incarceration. They didn't know much, but, as had been mentioned earlier, it involved her giving a female neighbor poison.

About that time, Miss Sophia, who had heard them talking, jumped in and explained. "When Alejandro and I picked up our bus tickets, the agent informed us there would be a recently released ex-con traveling on this bus."

Miss Sophia immediately did a Google search and read all about Edith. After Edith had been imprisoned for ten years, the neighbor's husband was found guilty of poisoning his wife. It was determined that Edith had nothing to do with it. Edith was immediately discharged.

Edith now shared with Miss Sophia that she had been wrongfully imprisoned for something she had not done. For ten years every day, she fought for her innocence. It was extremely tough, struggling not to give up and take a plea deal. Edith told her, "With God's help and the bishop's belief in me, I survived."

Miss Sophia started to cry, and when she looked up at the three young men, they had tears in their eyes too. Someone handed her a tissue. Miss Sophia said, "I can't imagine. I cannot imagine," and the young men agreed. Miss Sophia further explained that Edith was now suing for false imprisonment, which would most likely be settled. This settlement should net her a great deal of money.

Bishop Burrell had believed Edith the entire time she was incarcerated, and they had become really close friends. Edith had been released approximately six months ago but wasn't ready to leave Tennessee. When she decided it was time to rebuild a life for herself, Bishop Burrell had agreed to go with her and help her get back on her feet. He agreed to help her get settled back into society.

After that story, Michael felt like he had a lot of explaining to do. He shared with them why he was on this trip to Kansas City, about Jordan, their tracking strips invention, and the M&J Technology Company.

Michael told them all about the money in the suitcase, and the bishop's plan to entice the robbers to retrieve Michael's luggage and their loot, to identify them. He also explained how he was assisting the police in recovering the stolen money by using his tracking strip system. They thought this was very intriguing yet were shocked by how all of this was going on right under their noses.

As things began settling back down, Michael started thinking more about Risk, Time, and Money equals Reward. He and Jordan had risked a lot by stepping out and obtaining a business loan for the start-up of M&J Technology. They had invested nearly three years of their life in developing their products and building their company's infrastructure to get it to this point. Now was the time to engage investors to further the advancement of their company, no matter if it was short-term or long-term investors. They had a great product, and this recent episode reconfirmed to Michael that their next step would be acquiring interested investors.

CHAPTER **8**

Medical Emergency

The passengers on the bus settled back into their seats, and some even nodded off to sleep. Jayden leaned on Dr. Abernathy's arm, and it pleased the doctor that Jayden had accepted him.

Then, all of a sudden, approximately five police cars and two ambulances, with lights flashing and sirens blaring, rapidly approached the bus. This commotion woke and startled the passengers on the bus and they seemed to be concerned. Now what? All the vehicles sped right past the bus without slowing down one bit. The passengers were all a little relieved that the police were not after their bus, but then realized something severe must have happened up ahead.

As they neared the incident, traffic started to back up on the highway. The bus driver noticed a policeman, and he yelled out of his window to him. The officer came over and said, "One of our cars and a fleeing vehicle both rolled over during a police chase. The officer and a female sustained serious injuries."

Dr. Abernathy stood up and said to the officer, "I'm a doctor. Would you like me to assist?"

The officer replied, "Yes, come with me."

Dr. Abernathy glanced back at Edward, who was now checking on Jayden, and said, "I'll be fine."

Dr. Abernathy asked the bus driver to accompany him to the luggage compartment. He needed to get medical supplies from a container he had brought. As Dr. Abernathy and the bus driver were exiting the bus, Nathan stood up and asked Dr. Abernathy if he could assist him. Dr. Abernathy said, "Absolutely, follow me."

Johnathan and Michael were excited that Nathan wanted to step up and do this. Both of them gave him hugs and high fives as he left the bus. Everyone else on the bus immediately moved to the right side of the bus, to watch what was happening. Bishop Burrell decided to put his clergy collar on before getting off the bus and going to check things out for himself.

The bishop walked over and observed two police officers had a young man cuffed and restrained in the back of their police vehicle. They were reading him his Miranda Rights, and when the man voluntarily agreed to cooperate, they began questioning him about the money in his trunk. They advised him that they had retrieved a suitcase from his trunk, and upon inspecting its contents, they found a large sum of cash. They also determined that this money was from the same bank that had recently been held up.

The young man told the police that he was not involved in any of this, nor did he know anything about a bank robbery. He was sobbing, overcome by the possible loss of his wife in this auto accident.

The story he told the police, as overheard by Bishop Burrell, didn't add up in the bishop's mind. So, Bishop Burrell walked over to the police and said directly to the young man, "It's time for you to come clean."

The young man scowled at the bishop, but then noticed that he was a man of the cloth, and he immediately began revealing the truth. It appeared that previously, this young man and his wife had been approached by two men in a Walmart parking lot, back in Memphis. Those men were carrying a package with a bundle of money and asked the man and his wife if they would be willing to transport this money to Kansas City for them. If they did this, without any problems, the two men would pay them ten thousand dollars.

Even though these two men were relatively well dressed, this request sounded very strange. But the young man and his wife needed the money and decided to take the risk and do it.

After agreeing to do this, the young man and his wife realized they had to find some way to get the package to Kansas City without being caught with the money.

As they were driving back to their apartment, they came up with a plan to get the package to Kansas City safely. They dreamed up a scheme to secretly off-load the money into someone's luggage destined for Kansas City, Missouri. Being a private car driver, all the young man would need to do is wait for a fare that would fit the situation. He would then place the money into the passenger's luggage without the person's knowledge.

Soon, the young man got a request from a Michael Bell for a trip to go to the bus station. He asked Michael where he was headed, and as luck would have it, Michael indicated he was going to Kansas City. Now, all the young man had to do was place the money into Michael's luggage without being discovered. He and his wife would trail the bus to Kansas City and figure out a way to retrieve luggage with the money in it.

"The two men at the Walmart said they would contact us within a week and arrange to meet up and transfer the money," the young man explained. "Once we turned the money over to the two men, they said we would receive our ten thousand dollars. You know, I kind of thought those guys were probably watching my wife and me. It was just a hunch."

All the pieces were beginning to fall into place, with the information Michael had shared with the bishop and what he had experienced. The policeman told the young man that if he would help them find the real bank robbers, he might be able to plea bargain a lighter sentence for his involvement in concealing a crime, fleeing, and eluding the police.

The police stated, "He had better hope no one dies."

The young man agreed to do all he could, but asked, "Can I see my wife first? I need to see if she is okay."

The police officers thanked Bishop Burrell and quickly left to take the young man to check on his wife.

By the time the bishop returned to the bus, Dr. Abernathy had already gathered the things he needed from his medical container, such as stethoscopes, facial masks, and latex gloves. The bus driver was instructed to leave his container accessible because the doctor might require additional supplies after he assessed the situation.

Wasting no time, Dr. Abernathy and Nathan went to the accident scene. The area looked like a mess. A car had lost control, crashed into a guardrail, and flipped over several times. The police vehicle had subsequently slammed into it, flipped over, and come to rest on the edge of a steep embankment. The crashed police vehicle was hanging on the edge of a steep drop-off leading down to a riverbank. The police were trying to prevent the car from slipping into the river while removing the injured officer from the vehicle.

Other police officers were roping off the area and taking photographs and measurements. The police were also assisting the emergency technicians with the injured.

Dr. Abernathy and Nathan approached the EMTs, introduced themselves, and asked how they could help. The lead EMT indicated there had been a police chase, and two people in that car were suspected bank robbers. The officer was injured and pinned inside his patrol car. The female had been ejected from her vehicle.

Dr. Abernathy decided that he would check out the wounded officer himself, and Nathan should go over and check out the female. The EMTs indicated that they thought the female had already died. Nathan immediately went to assess her condition.

When Nathan approached the area where the female was, he noticed that she was already on a gurney and had a white sheet placed over her. Nathan asked if he could see her. The EMT proceeded to lift the sheet, and Nathan stepped forward to take a look. Nathan bent over and took his stethoscope, moving it all about the woman's body, even her ankles, checking for any signs of life. Nathan stood up and said, "She's still alive, but she has some serious internal injuries."

Nathan told the EMTs, "We must move swiftly and get her to the nearest hospital."

The EMTs looked at each other and realized there was no time to question this, and they immediately loaded the woman into the ambulance and administered oxygen. It was going to take a good thirty minutes to get the woman to the nearest hospital. Nathan said Dr. Abernathy should also assess this situation.

Dr. Abernathy immediately reviewed Nathan's findings and told the EMTs that Nathan was correct. He also asked Nathan if he would go with them. Nathan agreed to go. The woman's husband was thrilled to know that his wife was alive and on her way to the hospital. The police also decided to take him to the hospital.

Two journalists on-site took pictures and asked questions of the EMTs and Dr. Abernathy. Dr. Abernathy indicated that right now, he was too busy. He added that they should be speaking to the police and not him.

Word got back to the bus of what Nathan had determined, and that he had left in one of the ambulances. Johnathan was a little concerned about his brother being rushed off in an ambulance. Michael knew that he could track where Nathan was going because he had placed a tracking strip on Nathan's neck while he hugged him when exiting the bus earlier. Johnathan thought that was awesome, and he also checked his neck for a tracking strip.

By the time Dr. Abernathy got back down the hill, to where the injured police officer's vehicle was, the EMTs and police had cut the officer out of the car and had him lying on a gurney. They had had to use the Jaws of Life tool because the police officer was trapped inside his car. They had pried open the door of the vehicle and pulled the officer out right before the car slid down the embankment and splashed into the river.

The officer had a large open gash over his right eye, which was going to require many stitches. For now, they applied butterfly bandages on it to help hold it together and stop the bleeding. They were more concerned that the officer had a possible spinal injury and significant damage to his lower right leg. He was screaming that he couldn't move or feel his feet and toes.

Dr. Abernathy and the EMTs discussed that the injured police officer looked like he might have severed the tibia and fibula bones in his leg. Dr. Abernathy asked if they had any methylprednisolone or any other anti-inflammatory drugs, or a spinal board.

The EMTs said, "No, we don't, but we wish we did."

Dr. Abernathy paused a moment and told one of the EMTs and a police officer to follow him to the bus. When they got to the bus, the bus driver was standing outside. He said, "How can I help?"

Dr. Abernathy replied, "We need the surfboard that's in the luggage compartment."

"Oh, that's Johnathan's," said the bus driver.

The EMT jumped on the bus and asked Johnathan if they could use his surfboard. "Sure, definitely," Johnathan responded, really not knowing why they needed it.

Then, Dr. Abernathy stepped into the bus and yelled, "Anybody that has a belt, we need it!" He looked at Edith and said, "If you have any more of those marijuana cookies, I need at least two." Edith looked over at Bishop Burrell, and he indicated by nodding his head that it was okay.

Dr. Abernathy, the EMTs, and the police officer took the surfboard, cookies, and belts, then headed back down the hill to the injured police officer. In a few minutes, they were back up the hill with the injured police officer strapped to the top of the surfboard. The injured police officer wasn't screaming anymore; in fact, he seemed very relaxed on top of the surfboard.

Dr. Abernathy said, "Let's get him to the hospital right away," and told the EMTs that he would go with them to the hospital before autonomic dysreflexia might set in, which can cause high blood pressure or a slow heart rate. Dr. Abernathy added, "Let's get his blood pressure and heart monitor connected." He said that they were going to need everything they had to save this officer's life.

One of the police officers came over and informed the bus driver that Dr. Abernathy was going to the hospital in the other ambulance. Then, almost immediately, everyone looked at Michael.

Edward asked, "Did you put a tracking strip on my father?"

Michael said, "Well . . . I did put one on my belt."

Everyone cheered with glee and asked Michael to keep them informed. They told Michael how great his and Jordan's invention was. Alejandro spoke up and said, "This device is a little eerie on the privacy issue but can be appreciated in many useful situations such as this."

Now, here is where things really got crazy. Several of the passengers got very emotional and cried. All this appeared to happen suddenly and inexplicably.

Maria began sharing that her husband had died two years ago in Iraq, when Jayden was only five, and that it had been a tough time. Maria was traveling to Kansas City for an audition at the Kauffman Center for the Performing Arts. If she did not get accepted there, she would need to return to Texas, so she and Jayden could be closer to family. Maria said that she had never been interested in dating anyone until she saw Edward smile at her.

Victoria also was very emotional; she shared that the father of her baby wanted nothing to do with her or the unborn infant. Everyone on the bus was surprised at this because all along they had assumed Alejandro was the baby's father. In fact, Victoria and Alejandro had only met about two months ago. He had insisted on accompanying her on this trip, and on supporting her traveling to her sister's home. She wanted to have her baby there.

Alejandro shared that he had come to the United States to do research on environmental issues. In the process, he had met Victoria. He confessed that he was not Puerto Rican or Prince, the entertainer; in fact, he was a real prince. Everyone gasped and then started laughing.

Alejandro said he was actually next in line to be the king of a small island off the coast of Maui, Hawaii, called Malanai, known for its pineapples and seafood. Alejandro wanted to improve this island by stimulating its economy through greenhouse farms and building self-sustaining ecosystems powered by solar energy.

Alejandro informed the passengers that Miss Sophia was his aunt and protector. She was the deeded owner of the entire island. Her father, before he died, had left her the island and made her brother, Alejandro's father, king. Miss Sophia was quite wealthy, so she was the one to get to know.

By now, the police had cleared a path for the bus to exit the accident area. The bus driver decided to go pick up Dr. Abernathy and Nathan from the Missouri Medical Hospital. Their location was traced by Michael's tracking strips on Nathan's neck and Michael's belt used on the rescue board of the injured police officer.

CHAPTER **9**

7-Eleven

After all of the excitement, a restroom break was needed. The bus driver announced they would be stopping soon at a 7-Eleven just up the road. If they needed to go to the restroom or get a snack, they would have to do it quickly, because they were way behind schedule and needed to get back on the road.

When the bus arrived at the 7-Eleven, it was late afternoon, and the parking lot was empty. The bus driver decided to top off his fuel tank since this 7-Eleven had a special diesel pump for trucks and buses.

Of course, all the women immediately got out and headed for the restroom. Edward told Maria he would stay on the bus because he did not want to wake Jayden.

The guys trickled in and out, except for Michael. He told the bus driver he was going to run over to the Liquor Shop near the 7-Eleven. He wanted to see if they carried Bell Blended Bourbon, his liquor of choice.

While in the Liquor Shop, Michael went to the restroom and then browsed through the shop. Sure enough, they had a bottle of *BBB*. Michael chatted with the shop owner about being the son of the owner of Bell Blended Bourbon.

Meanwhile, everyone was getting back on the bus when Jayden woke up. Now, he needed to go to the restroom. So much for a quick pit stop. Edward told Maria that he would take Jayden inside to the restroom.

While Edward and Jayden were in the restroom, two men pulled up in front of the 7-Eleven and jumped out of their car. The bus driver and the bishop noticed and thought something looked suspicious. They watched these two characters through the front windows and could see they appeared to be robbing the 7-Eleven.

The men screamed at the store clerk to open the cash drawer and hand over all the money. They waved their guns and shouted very loudly, telling the store clerk to, "Open the fucking cash drawer, and if you don't, I'm going to blow your stupid head off."

The bishop had never carried a gun the whole time he was employed at the prison, but that did not stop him from getting involved. The bus driver, on the other hand, was licensed to carry a gun, and he was not opposed to using it when necessary. He pulled out his Smith & Wesson .357 Magnum revolver. He then directed everyone to move to the back of the bus and stay down. Johnathan and Alejandro made sure everyone got down and took shelter.

While all this was going on, Edward and Jayden were in the restroom. He could hear the commotion and shouting in the store. Edward told Jayden to get in the toilet stall, lock the door, and not come out until he came back to get him. Jayden could tell that he was very serious. Jayden did exactly what Edward told him to do. He even climbed up on the back of the toilet and crouched against the back wall.

Edward slipped out of the restroom to investigate what was going on, and to make sure no one else on the bus was in trouble. Edward could see that the two thugs were up to no good. These two men became very aggravated with the store clerk taking so much time, and kept telling him to hurry up.

Edward overheard them scream, "Motherfucker, you better not be alarming the police, or you're a dead man!"

The store clerk frantically opened the cash drawer and stuffed the money into a brown paper bag. One of the men raised his gun and shot the store clerk in the middle of his forehead. Edward had seen violence like this before when he was growing up, and it never ended well. In a flash, Edward recalled when he was only five years old, and his father was doing his residency at the New York City Hospital in Harlem. He, his mother, and father had gone to a local grocery store to do their weekly shopping. Edward and his father were in the back of the store, looking for one last item his mother insisted on getting.

When a man came into the store, he got enraged over something, pulled out a gun, and started shooting. The next thing Edward recalled was his father pushing him into a back room and then running toward the front of the store. Edward remembered being ushered to the front and then outside by a store clerk. When Edward passed the checkout, there was his mother lying on the floor with blood all over her. His father looked like he was trying to save her.

Edward heard his father screaming at his mother, "Anita, Anita!" His mother died that day, and his father had to become both mother and father. Edward would sometimes just sit alone on his bed and cry into a pillow because he didn't want his father to hear and be upset. Over the years, his father poured himself into his work, and because of that, their relationship became strained. Edward had thought that his father wanted to take this bus trip so they might work on rebuilding their relationship.

Right now, Edward knew he needed to address this situation, and not anger the robbers any further. He tried to be quiet in the store, but the other robber discovered him anyway. He told Edward to get up front and asked him if anyone else was with him. Edward said, "No, I'm alone."

The robber forced Edward toward the front door, using him as a shield as they made their getaway. Edward tried to go along and cooperate, moving them further away from Jayden. When the robbers pushed Edward past the front counter, he saw blood spattered on the countertop and droplets of blood with skin tissue all over the cigarette case behind the counter.

The scene almost made Edward nauseous, but he knew he needed to hold it together.

Meanwhile, Miss Sophia, on the bus, had called 911. She told them what the situation was, identified herself, and described how frightened all the passengers were. The 911 operator instructed Miss Sophia to stay on the phone, try to remain calm, and reassured her the police were on their way.

Bishop Burrell stripped off his clergy collar and bolted into action. He knew God would be with him as he got off the bus. He positioned himself by the side of the sliding front doors. When the two robbers came outside with Edward in front of them, the bishop cold-cocked the man that was holding Edward. Stunned, the robber released Edward, and immediately he fell to the ground. The other robber raised his gun and shot at Bishop Burrell. The bullet grazed the bishop's right shoulder.

Quickly, the bus driver sprang out of the bus, and without hesitation, shot both men in their knees, point-blank. They fell to the ground screaming and moaning. The bus driver ran over to them and told them, "Don't move, or I'll shoot you sons of bitches again." He quickly grabbed their guns, gave one to the bishop, and told him to watch them while he got something to tie them up. The driver said, "If they move a muscle, shoot 'em."

Edward immediately got up and headed back to the restroom to check on Jayden. Maria, exiting the bus, frantically screamed, "Where is Jayden?" She ran to Edward as he entered the store.

When they got to the men's restroom, the stall door was still locked. Edward looked over the top of the stall and saw Jayden. Thank God, he had not moved. Edward told Jayden everything was all right, and to come on out.

When Jayden opened the stall door, his mom grabbed him up in a huge hug that lasted at least five minutes. Edward and Maria both praised how brave Jayden was and said how proud they were of him.

By the time they exited the store, the police had arrived. The police officers questioned the bus driver and Bishop Burrell. They also quickly took statements from everyone else while the EMTs treated the bishop's shoulder. Maria informed Edward that she and Jayden needed to sit in their seats for right now. Edward was a little confused but respected Maria enough to give her some space.

While Michael was in the Liquor Shop, they heard police and ambulance sirens all around that area. So, Michael and the shop owner stepped out of the store, and to Michael's surprise, the parking lot of the 7-Eleven looked like a war zone. He walked over to the bus driver and said, "What the hell happened?"

Michael could sense the bus driver was taken aback by what had just occurred here. He quickly gave him a brief explanation and told Michael to get back on the bus.

Everyone now boarded the bus and got back in their seats. When the bus driver stepped back onto the bus, everyone applauded with cheers of appreciation for how the bus driver and Bishop Burrell had controlled and subdued the two thugs. The word "hero" was used for the bus driver, bishop, Edward, and yes, Jayden.

The bus driver announced, "Okay, no more stops. We're headed straight to the hospital." It was clear that nobody was going to argue with the bus driver after what he did at the 7-Eleven.

The bus driver couldn't figure out whether it was all of the excitement that exhausted everyone, or if the passengers just needed time to reflect. Either way, the bus was quiet during the entire ride to the hospital.

CHAPTER 10

Hospital and More

When they reached the hospital, the bus driver pulled up to the emergency room parking area and told Johnathan and Edward to go into the hospital to locate their brother and father. As they were exiting the bus, they stopped and asked Bishop Burrell to go along with them. Edward suggested that if the bishop put his clergy collar back on, they would stand a better chance of getting help right away.

After the men left the bus, the bus driver pulled into the visitor's parking lot.

Upon entering the emergency room, the bishop went right over to the admissions desk and explained they were looking for Dr. Robert Abernathy and Dr. Nathan Willis. He said they were family members. That was the first time Johnathan heard someone call his brother a doctor. It was awesome.

The nurse looked at her computer and told them to have a seat; it might be a while because Dr. Abernathy was currently with a patient in the main building. She indicated she would try paging him, but they could wait in the waiting room area. She also advised them that Dr. Willis was currently in surgery and could not be disturbed.

The bishop called the bus driver and told him what was going on. He indicated he didn't know how long it would be before they could see Dr. Abernathy or Dr. Willis.

While everyone was waiting, Alejandro and Victoria went into the emergency room and asked to meet privately with Bishop Burrell. They pulled him to the side and assembled in one of the counseling rooms. They said they wanted the bishop to marry them before the baby was born. They met for about thirty minutes, and with much arm-twisting, he finally agreed.

The bishop was concerned that they might be rushing into this marriage. They explained they had already acquired a marriage license from the recorder's office at the Historic Truman Courthouse in Independence, Missouri. Their previous plans had been to get married at Victoria's sister's house next Saturday.

When the bishop agreed, Victoria got so excited that she immediately walked over to the nurses' station and inquired if they had a chapel in the hospital. She was hoping the bishop could marry her and Alejandro there.

The nurse noticed that Victoria looked like she was very close to delivering and joked, "Well, I think we better hurry. Let me check with my manager and see if it's available. I'll be right back."

At that moment, Dr. Abernathy stepped out of the elevator with a male nurse's aide, carrying the surfboard and belts. The nurse's aide gave Michael the belts and Alejandro the surfboard, but none of these belts belonged to Michael. Michael's mother had gifted him with a very expensive Salvatore Ferragamo belt with an estimated value of around $400 for his graduation. He had wanted to look his best and wear it to Kansas City for this critical business trade show. At the moment, Michael did not make an issue of the missing belt, given all that was happening.

Edward immediately rushed over to his father and hugged him. He asked him if he was all right.

"Yes, I'm just fine," Dr. Abernathy answered. The doctor also thanked Johnathan for allowing them to use his surfboard.

Dr. Abernathy shared that it immediately became apparent to him why the EMTs insisted on traveling all the way to the Missouri Medical Hospital. This hospital was a very progressive hospital that not only had made refurbishments to an existing facility and campus but had also fully integrated new medical technologies and advanced patient care.

Dr. Abernathy continued to explain what had happened. With this hospital's state-of-the-art equipment and knowledgeable staff, they had been able to diagnose the officer's situation quickly. He required twenty-three stitches over his right eye, but they left the right corner with a butterfly bandage, so his eye would blink properly. The officer had severed the two bones in his lower right leg. It required them to attach two titanium rods to the broken bones using thirty-six titanium bolts to rebuild his leg.

The good news, other than his leg, was that the officer most likely was going to come through this without any spinal cord damage. Also, they determined that he had strained his back muscles, and would require physical therapy. The officer was going to remain in the hospital for several days while in treatment. The hospital staff indicated that the quick use of the surfboard and the anchoring of his leg, thus immobilizing it, had minimized the officer's injuries. Oh yes, and the use of the marijuana cookies had been genius.

The hospital felt that, after three months of recovery, the officer should be able to get back to work. It was great news for him and his family.

The other injured person, the female, was still in surgery. Nathan had been asked to assist on the surgical team. They were astounded that he had been able to detect her internal injuries. There was a lot of talk about what a great doctor he was going to become.

Dr. Abernathy indicated that he had been released to go, but they needed to wait on Nathan to finish up in the operating room.

The bishop said, "Well, then we've got time for a wedding!"

Dr. Abernathy immediately looked at Edward, and Edward responded, "No, not me. He's talking about Alejandro and Victoria."

About this time, the nurse shared with Victoria that they could not use the chapel. She suggested the beautiful garden area out back instead, near a reflecting pool. The area would be well-lit at this time of day.

Victoria turned to Alejandro and said, "I think that would be great."

The bishop called the bus driver once again and asked him to pull the bus up to the emergency room door and pick them up. He told the bus driver that they wanted to go around to the rear of the hospital, by the reflecting pool. Everyone on the bus was invited to join Alejandro and Victoria in their marriage ceremony!

By the time they exited the emergency room door, the bus had just pulled up. Maria, Edith, and Miss Sophia were already outside picking flowers from the landscape around the building to make a bouquet for Victoria. The bus driver took the surfboard and returned it to the luggage compartment. He then drove the bus to the other side of the hospital's garden area.

On the way to the garden area, Bishop Burrell opened his briefcase, which included the marriage license that Alejandro had given him and some legal documents Miss Sophia had provided. Then he explained a few legal details of their marriage. Alejandro and Victoria sat down and signed the marriage documents. Actually, now, they were legally married.

At this time, everyone proceeded to the garden wedding ceremony area. All the guests gathered around in the garden. It was indeed a beautiful night with the lights bouncing off the water around the reflecting pool. The evening was magical, and every star in the sky began to shine brightly. You could definitely use the word "perfect."

Victoria and Alejandro asked Maria and Edward to sing a song for them and to stand up with them as their maid of honor and best man. This situation brought Edward and Maria back together. Maria shared with Edward that the whole 7-Eleven event had scared her about possibly losing Jayden and him.

Victoria's contractions had now begun and were increasing in intensity. Understanding this, Bishop Burrell quickly moved through the marriage ceremony.

During the ring portion, Alejandro pulled out a ring that had an exotic eight-millimeter black pearl set in the center, surrounded with eighteen triple-excellent diamonds. This ring had previously belonged to Miss Sophia. It had been given to her by her family's elders. Miss Sophia was proud it would now belong to Alejandro's wife. Later, Miss Sophia would explain that the black pearl was a symbol of hope and that some believe it protects the wearer from negative energy.

During the ceremony, strangely, Maria and Edward stared at each other and repeated the vows silently along with Alejandro and Victoria. Jayden noticed and loved this, so he walked up and took his mom's right hand in his left hand and Edward's left hand in his right and completed the circle.

After the ceremony was over, Jayden asked, "Are we married yet?"

Maria and Edward laughed and said, "Not yet, but maybe soon."

As they were walking away, Jayden walked up to Dr. Abernathy and said, "We're not married yet." Dr. Abernathy said, "I'm sure it will be soon."

On the way back to the bus, Victoria and Alejandro stopped to kiss, while everyone took pictures with their cell phones. Michael opened the bottle of bourbon he had bought earlier and poured the bourbon into some small paper cups he had also purchased. Everyone lifted their cups for a toast to the bride and groom. Everyone took a drink, except the driver, Jayden, and Victoria. They, of course, couldn't have any.

All of a sudden, Victoria announced her water just broke. Dr. Abernathy said, "Well, it's a good thing we're here. Hurry. Get back on the bus, and let's get Victoria to the emergency room."

When Dr. Abernathy, Miss Sophia, Victoria, and Alejandro reentered the emergency room, the nurses knew why. The head nurse said, "Are you married now, and are you ready to have your baby?" They all laughed as she pulled up a wheelchair for Victoria to sit.

CHAPTER 11

Departures

The head nurse informed Victoria of hospital policy, whereby she could not wear any of her jewelry during her delivery in the hospital. With some reluctance, she removed her wedding ring and asked Miss Sophia to hold onto it for her. She commented, "I'm going to want this back."

The nurse asked Alejandro if he wanted to come along with his wife, and without hesitation, he joined them in the elevator. Alejandro made a comment, "Wife and baby in a matter of hours. Wow, my life is moving fast." Alejandro smiled at Victoria as she began experiencing another intense labor pain.

The head nurse in the emergency room suggested that Dr. Abernathy and Miss Sophia go to the maternity ward, where there was a large waiting room. Dr. Abernathy and Miss Sophia exited the emergency room door and walked towards the main building.

A television camera crew and many journalists were waiting just outside the front door. As Dr. Abernathy passed, one of the reporters asked, "Aren't you Dr. Abernathy?" He responded, "Well, yes, I am."

A reporter with a microphone asked, "Can I talk to you about what you know in connection with a recent bank robbery? You know, the one with the police chase that injured two people, one of whom was a police officer?"

Dr. Abernathy responded, "I don't know any details regarding a bank robbery. I am aware that the police recovered the stolen money. I believe a company called M&J Technology assisted the police in solving that case. You should speak to a gentleman by the name of Michael Bell, from Memphis, Tennessee. He should be able to furnish you with more details. Concerning the injured people, you'll need to talk to the hospital administration. I might add, an extremely talented doctor by the name of Nathan Willis assisted the EMTs."

Then Dr. Abernathy walked away and joined Miss Sophia in locating the maternity ward waiting room. While they looked for the waiting room, Dr. Abernathy called the bus driver and told him what had happened. He suggested it might be a good idea to avoid the reporters on his way up.

One might have thought that Miss Sophia was the grandmother, and in fact, that was almost what it was. Miss Sophia had watched over Alejandro since he was ten years old, after his mother's death. She loved him and knew she would love Victoria and the new baby.

Everyone gathered in the maternity waiting room, including the bus driver. In one corner, Johnathan and Miss Sophia were engaged in a conversation, discussing finances. Edward and Maria shared their past experiences, while the bus driver decided to catch a quick nap.

Edith brought the last batch of non-cannabis cookies for everyone in their group to enjoy while in the waiting room.

Dr. Abernathy used most of his time to catch up on phone calls.

Michael wandered off to get himself a drink, and while at the vending machines, struck up a conversation with an attractive female nurse. He asked if he could call her. She was flattered and gave him her name, Chloe Johnson, and phone number.

Chloe accompanied Michael to the gift shop and helped him pick out a baby gift. It was a snow globe of Kansas City. He thought the baby could then remember where he or she was born. Chloe was impressed by Michael's thoughtfulness.

Nathan joined them, and they caught him up on all the recent events. He shared that the car driver had cooperated with the police, and the man had apologized for putting the money in Michael's suitcase. He seemed to be extremely appreciative of Nathan's help in saving his wife's life.

Nathan indicated to the group that he and Johnathan would stick around at the hospital after they saw the new baby. Nathan wanted to discuss with Johnathan the opportunities that had been offered to him. The hospital administrator had just offered the possibility of transferring Nathan's residency to the Missouri Medical Hospital. This offer could present many more opportunities for him in the future. Nathan said he would need to get a rental car to use during their stay here in Kansas City.

Dr. Abernathy asked Nathan if he could have a private moment with him, and of course, Nathan said yes. Dr. Abernathy said, "What an outstanding job you did." He looked directly into Nathan's eyes and said, "Did you see it first, or hear it?" Nathan responded, "I saw it."

Dr. Abernathy said, "You got the Gift. Don't let anyone or anything distract you."

Then, Alejandro came out to share, "It's a boy! And Victoria is doing great. His name is Asera Theodore Kamealoha, which means 'Lucky gift of beloved one.'" Then there were hugs and high fives all around.

Alejandro indicated his secret service personnel would be taking over from here, and that he, Miss Sophia, Victoria, and Asera, would be departing in a few days for Malanai.

Alejandro invited everyone to the nursery viewing area for a peek at Asera. Upon seeing the baby, you could tell on Victoria, Alejandro, and Miss Sophia's faces that he was going to bring so much joy to their lives.

Michael gave Asera's gift to Alejandro. Laughingly, Alejandro said, "Does this have a tracker on it?"

Michael said, "I could put one on it if you want me to."

Alejandro indicated that he would like that. It would allow them to stay in touch with each other.

Dr. Abernathy then announced that he would be departing soon. His brother, the governor of Kansas, would be picking him up. Edward could make his own choices as to what he wanted to do. Dr. Abernathy said, "I'm very proud of my son and the great choices he has been making."

Of course, Edward chose to stay with Maria and Jayden. It was the first time Maria had heard that Edward's uncle was the governor of Kansas. She wondered what other surprises Edward might not have shared with her yet.

Edward, Maria, Jayden, and Michael decided to share an Uber ride to the Aladdin Hotel. The hotel was conveniently located right around the corner from the Kansas City Conference Center, where Michael's trade show was being held, and the Kauffman Center for the Performing Arts. This arrangement would work well for all of them.

After a quick visit to the nursery, everyone returned to the bus to retrieve their luggage, except Michael. His luggage, of course, had been stolen and was now in evidence at the police station. Michael had not thought about this, but he now had to buy himself some clothes, including a belt and personal supplies. As everyone was departing, Michael intuitively knew these people were going to be in his life in the future, somehow.

The bus driver, Edith, and Bishop Burrell headed to the bus station, then to their final destination; during this time, everyone else had already departed. The bus driver felt this had been one of the most memorable trips he had ever taken, and he looked forward to the next adventure.

CHAPTER 12

Business Heightens

After Michael settled in his hotel room, he received a phone call from Jordan. He sounded anxious. "Where have you been, and what in the hell is going on?"

It seemed that the media were covering stories about the M&J Technology Company, and the company's phone had been ringing continuously. Michael told Jordan to sit down because he had an unbelievable story to share with him. After an hour or more on the phone, he and Jordan agreed that tomorrow's trade show was perfect timing.

The next morning, by the time Michael arrived at the trade show check-in station, he was informed that the only booth remaining was number thirteen, so that was where they set him up. The registrar sarcastically laughed and said, "Hope that doesn't bother you."

Michael said, "No, not at all! You see, I believe you need to pursue your own luck." The registrar said, "Do you really believe that?"

Michael smiled at him and said, "Yes, I definitely do!"

In fact, when Michael got to his booth, there were investors and resellers anxiously waiting to talk to him. The recent media coverage had heightened the interest of a large number of potential investors in M&J products. The investors anticipated Michael would share the concepts of M&J Technology at this trade show.

Michael spoke with many investors about the M&J Technology Company's business plan, including cybersecurity, technology efficiencies, and supply- chain effectiveness. A lot of investors showed great interest in their unique products. Several investors requested additional proof of concept associated with the live-tracking application and questioned the reliability of its functionality. They suggested the products be put through additional and complete validation before investing.

Unfortunately, Michael and Jordan did not have many real examples other than the recent bank robbery situation. One thing Michael had learned was, you should not always assume as fact what appears to be obvious. He could thank Bishop Burrell for that.

Michael had come to realize that some investors need to be fully assured and convinced before they take chances with their money. They also wanted to understand how much M&J Technology would be personally invested in this project. Michael had to think through his plan of how he could validate his products to these investors. He knew in his heart, and by way of beta testing that these products were rock solid.

Later that evening, Michael felt he had hit a roadblock in his quest to acquire investors. Michael decided to go down to the Martini Loft in his hotel, have a drink, try to relax, and develop a strategy. The investors had proved to be tough to win over.

Michael arrived at the bar in the lobby with his briefcase and ordered a vodka martini straight up with three olives. He carried his briefcase with him nearly everywhere he went. While enjoying his drink, Michael started reading local Kansas City news articles from his laptop about how the M&J tracking strip had assisted in locating a large sum of money. This money was part of a recent robbery of the Memphis Plains Bank.

Michael then observed another alarming article describing the murders of two nurses from the Missouri Medical Hospital. Both nurses had been choked by something other than a rope. The evidence relating to the murder weapon, i.e., bruising, scarring, etc., suggested the weapon could be some sort of a wide strap, such as a belt.

One of the nurses was identified as Chloe Johnson. Michael was stunned and sat, shocked, for a few minutes. Then, he thought, *Belt? Could this have been my belt?*

Michael quickly opened up the JAM app on his laptop. He called up the tracking strip he had previously attached to his belt. Sure enough, his belt had been in these girls' apartment.

Michael immediately contacted the police station and shared the information he had just discovered. The police were extremely eager for Michael to come in and demonstrate how the JAM app worked and how the belt could be tracked. The cops asked Michael if the app could tell them where the belt was presently located.

Michael said, "Certainly!" He not only could show them where the belt was located but was able to furnish them with the complete physical address.

Michael explained to them how Dr. Abernathy, a world-renowned heart surgeon, had personally been involved in a previous case, and the doctor would corroborate and validate Michael's story along with other police officers. He explained how his belt had also been used in the rescue of an injured police officer in a previous case.

The police were already aware of that case. What they were most interested in was solving this case. They wanted to retrieve the belt and identify who was in possession of it.

Based on the information provided by the JAM app, the police were able to obtain a search warrant. The police needed to locate the physical belt within the premises for it to become valid evidence and to support this case. While searching the premises identified by the JAM app, the police discovered the belt was located in the apartment of a nurse's aide from Missouri Medical Hospital. When the belt was later forensically tested, it had the fingerprints of both victims on the belt, but the other fingerprints were not the nurse's aide's fingerprints. It was determined that the fingerprints were the prints of the nurse's aide's roommate.

With further investigation of the nurse's aide's work schedule, it was determined he could not have been involved in these murders. The nurse's aide was not the one who stole the belt. It was discovered through videotapes that his roommate had taken the belt from the nurse's aide's desk while visiting him at the hospital. Later that evening, the roommate followed the nurses to their home. One of the nurses' neighbors noticed this individual chatting with the nurses. He was joking around with them and asked them if he could come in for a drink.

Because of Michael's rapid response, which led to the murderer through his tracking strip, now many law enforcement agencies were getting excited about how they could utilize the M&J tracking strip and JAM app. They envisioned many more practical uses for it. The number of applications appeared to be endless.

By the third morning of the trade show, the word was out about this miracle invention, and how the M&J Technology Company had, once again, assisted in solving a major criminal case. When Michael arrived at the trade show, there, sitting at his booth, was Johnathan.

Michael was a little surprised, but very glad to see his new friend. Johnathan shared that he was now working for Miss Sophia as a financial advisor. She wanted him to meet with Michael and negotiate a possible investment agreement. Miss Sophia had a lot of interest in investing in M&J Technology Company.

When Johnathan mentioned a potential offer of a half a million dollars, Michael almost passed out. He told Johnathan that he needed to talk this over with Jordan, but he secretly knew Jordan would be thrilled!

CHAPTER **13**

The Future

(9 years later)

Well, you might be wondering whatever happened to the passengers of Bus 208. These passengers were extraordinarily lucky, as they just happened to have found themselves aboard this unique bus trip.

Michael Bell
At the time of M&J Technology Company's Public Launch Party (MJTC, New York Stock Exchange code), they had over one hundred thousand customers. M&J was now producing approximately ten thousand tracking strips per day, and operating at full production capacity. At the M&J annual meeting, they announced that over fifty thousand tracking strip application solutions worldwide had been identified with assistance from the M&J products. These numbers had risen significantly as more and more police, sheriff, and security agencies implemented the use of these tracking strips.

Michael and Jordan were incredibly proud that their partnership enjoyed an excellent internal working relationship. This type of relationship is not typical of many other new technology partnership start-ups.

M&J Technology prepared for a new product launch consisting of a clear strip, which could track a body's vital signs in real-time when worn by a person. In cooperation with Dr. Nathan Willis, this tracking strip was developed for use during a pandemic. Miss Sophia's initial investment had been paid back in full, and she remained a happy stockholder. Michael was now happily married and had twin girls.

Michael and Jordan's families were each incredibly proud of their accomplishments. Both families and everyone who traveled on Bus 208 that particular day attended the M&J Technology Company's public launch celebration. They enjoyed a special toast with Bell Blended Bourbon in small paper cups. Oh yes, they even had a king, queen, and prince at their launch. That had to be a first.

Bishop Burrell

Since the bus trip, Bishop Burrell had been called to be a cardinal. He was now Cardinal Leonardo James Burrell and resided within Vatican City. This six foot seven inch, two-hundred-fifty-five pound cardinal was one to be noticed. He walked like a giant but had the heart of a teddy bear. Michael and the cardinal developed a very close relationship over the years, with Michael refusing to launch any new products before Cardinal Burrell first gave each a special blessing.

Edith Rogers

Edith Rogers became the owner of Online Cookie Company, with a net worth of two million dollars. And yes, she remained licensed to sell cannabis-infused cookies. Edith's large cookies were always served at all M&J corporate parties, as well as any other special events hosted by passengers of Bus 208.

Edith prevailed in her false imprisonment case and was awarded an undisclosed amount. One thing about Edith—she always looked forward and never backward. Edith told Cardinal Burrell, when he became pope, she was going to make him an awesome giant cookie and put BFF (Best Friends Forever) on top.

The cardinal gave Edith one of those glares and said, "Edith!" then laughed.

Alejandro, Victoria, and Asera Kamealoha

Alejandro, Victoria, and Asera took the titles of king, queen, and prince of Malanai. Alejandro and Victoria, once crowned king and queen, implemented movements to improve the economy of Malanai through vertical greenhouse farming. Given the limited space for farming on the island, and the conundrum of how the world would feed the burgeoning population, this method of food growth could prove to be very fruitful. Population forecasts suggest by the year 2023, this type of business could top six billion four hundred thousand dollars. In conjunction with this type of growing method, a self-sustaining ecosystem, powered by solar energy, transformed Malanai into a very profitable island.

Victoria and Asera both became naturalized citizens of Malanai.

Asera was a typical nine-year-old who loved anything technical. Alejandro legally adopted him and positioned him to be king one day. Asera often carried his snow globe, that Michael gave him, in his backpack. It helped to keep him grounded and of course he knew he could be tracked. Asera also had a little sister named Lori, a symbol of honor and victory. Asera loved her dearly.

Miss Sophia Kamealoha

Sophia continued her role as a philanthropist, as well as holding private investments all over the world. Sophia loved being a silent partner. She always said that she didn't need to be an active partner when she carried the purse.

Miss Sophia's wealth was terrific, but her pride and joy remained Alejandro and his family. Occasionally she had Edith ship her special cookies for her grandchildren.

Edward, Maria, and Jayden Abernathy

Maria was accepted at the Kauffman Center for the Performing Arts, but she instead decided to take a different course. She and Edward became the owners of the Fabulous Pizza Corporation, with many franchises. Maria worked with Johnathan Willis in the development of a business partnership between the Fabulous Pizza Corporation, Martinez Enterprises (Maria's parents' business), and Miss Sophia. This partnership proved to be very lucrative. They also hosted musical expos every year, inviting top headline performers, including many famous musicians.

Edward and Maria purchased the original spot of the Fabulous Pizza Restaurant, expanded it, and made it their first restaurant. To capture the unique experience they had on their first visit, they insisted that all future Fabulous Pizza Restaurant franchises must agree to adhere to the original décor, floor plan, and unique Sunday rules.

Money was tight when they first started, so they held their wedding ceremony at the original Fabulous Pizza restaurant. Dr. Abernathy and Jayden made sure this time, Edward and Maria were actually married.

By the way, Maria was the only person with whom Edward had shared what he had seen at the Fabulous Pizza when he returned to get Maria's sweater. Neither could explain what had happened, but they were certain it was real, just like a dream come true or a miracle. Everyone that was in the Fabulous Pizza Restaurant that day found luck. Call it a fluke or a miracle; it's up to you.

M&J Technology Company purchased the entire brownstone building on Riverside Drive. On the ground floor, Michael and Jordan's wives operated a Fabulous Pizza franchise. They adhered to the requirements of the franchise agreement but were granted a special dispensation. Out of respect for the history of the Italian Pizzeria that used to reside in that spot, they were allowed to add two Southern-style pizza pies to the menu, Southern fried chicken, and muffuletta pies.

Often, people from West Memphis, Arkansas, would visit specifically for these pies. Many customers said the place had a magical feel, and it kept bringing them back.

When Edward shared with Maria about the event that occurred in connection with the death of his mother, Maria thought back to the previous trauma they had experienced. That was the day at the 7-Eleven when Edward took Jayden to the restroom, and two thugs killed the store clerk. She couldn't even imagine what pain and anguish Edward must have experienced. Yet he was steadfast and focused in protecting Jayden.

Edward's actions made Maria love him even more. She was determined to encourage Edward and his father to mend and grow their relationship. The relationship between Edward, his father, and Jayden became very strong.

When Jayden turned seventeen years old, he pursued a professional soccer career.

Dr. Robert Abernathy

As a world-renowned cardiovascular surgeon, Dr. Abernathy performed over five thousand heart procedures throughout his career. Once he retired, he enjoyed fishing with his grandson, Jayden. Dr. Abernathy also loved attending Jayden's soccer matches. Oh yes, he checked off one of his bucket-list items, attending the Arkansas fishing tournament in Mammoth Spring.

Johnathan Willis

Johnathan became the owner of Willis International Investment Company, dealing with global high technology and essential aerospace defense. He married and had three boys (triplets), and a girl was on the way. Johnathan never used his surfboard again but kept it hanging in his office as a reminder of that day on the bus. It reminded him always to respect people you meet because you never know when or how a friendship might begin. Johnathan used M&J tracking strips on his children. He said it was nice to know where they were, especially when they were at an amusement park.

Dr. Nathan Willis

Nathan became one of the assistant national directors for the Office of Infectious Diseases and began preparations for the next pandemic. Nathan never married, but he loved visiting Johnathan's boys.

Bus Driver

The bus driver of Bus 208, also known as Steven Stone, became the proud owner of a charter bus company with the motto "If you're traveling on Bus 208, you most likely will arrive late, but it will be the trip of a lifetime."

Car Driver

The hired car driver received a ten-year sentence in connection with the bank robbery but was paroled after five years for good behavior. He and his wife never returned to a life of crime. His wife continued to be extremely grateful to Nathan for saving her life. She recovered completely.

Bank Robbers

Even though the two bank robbers were never found, all the stolen money was fully recovered.

Lucky and Mitzy

It has been proven time and time again that many animals possess unique Gifts of their own. Some can alarm or alert humans, and others exhibit a very loving spirit. In fact, in a recent trip of Bus 208, transporting disabled children to a camp in Arkansas, there were two small dogs on board. Steven, the bus driver, invited his friend Edith to join these passengers on this trip. She thought it would be another excellent opportunity to share her cookies.

When Edith offered her cookies to everyone, Lucky, a Jack Russell Terrier, pranced up the aisle and took a cookie. This funny dog made all the kids laugh. As Lucky proceeded back to her owner, she stopped and glanced at a Yorkshire Terrier named Mitzy.

At that moment, Mitzy realized she had better get her cookie. With Lucky and Mitzy on board, every one of the children experienced a time without pain, sadness, or fear of dying, only a little humor by two special dogs.

You see, everyone has the Gift.
It's a matter of, are they lucky enough to
realize it, and will they ultimately seize
that opportunity?

CHAPTER 14

Edith's Ultimate Oatmeal Chocolate Chip C●●KIES

Ingredients

- 3/4 cup butter, softened
- 1 cup packed brown sugar
- 1/2 cup granulated sugar
- 1 teaspoon baking powder
- 1/4 teaspoon baking soda
- 1/2 teaspoon sea salt
- 1/2 teaspoon ground cinnamon
- 1/8 teaspoon ground cloves OR 2 tablespoons of bourbon
- 2 eggs
- 1 teaspoon vanilla
- 1 3/4 cups all-purpose flour
- 2 cups old fashioned oats
- 1 cup Semi-Sweet Chocolate morsels

Instructions

1. Preheat oven to 375°.
2. In large mixing bowl, beat butter with mixer on medium for 30 sec.
3. Add brown sugar, granulated sugar, baking powder, baking soda, salt, cinnamon and cloves OR bourbon. Beat until combined with an electric mixer.
4. Beat in eggs and vanilla until combined.
5. Beat in flour slowly.
6. Stir in old fashioned oats and Chocolate Morsels with a wooden spoon.
7. Drop dough by rounded teaspoons 2 inches apart onto ungreased cookie sheets with parchment paper.
8. Bake for 8 to 10 minutes or until edges are golden. Let stand on cookie sheets for 1 minute.
9. Transfer to wire racks and let cool. Makes about 48 cookies.

coda

Made in the USA
Columbia, SC
29 November 2020